PRINCESS Kitty

The Copycat

by **Melody Mews**   illustrated by **Ellen Stubbings**

LITTLE SIMON

New York   London   Toronto   Sydney   New Delhi

LITTLE SIMON

An imprint of Simon & Schuster Children's Publishing Division
1230 Avenue of the Americas, New York, New York 10020
First Little Simon hardcover edition June 2021. Copyright © 2021 by Simon & Schuster, Inc.
All rights reserved, including the right of reproduction in whole or in part in any form.
LITTLE SIMON is a registered trademark of Simon & Schuster, Inc., and associated colophon is a trademark of Simon & Schuster, Inc. For information about special discounts for bulk purchases, please contact Simon & Schuster Special Sales at 1-866-506-1949 or business@simonandschuster.com.
The Simon & Schuster Speakers Bureau can bring authors to your live event. For more information or to book an event contact the Simon & Schuster Speakers Bureau at 1-866-248-3049 or visit our website at www.simonspeakers.com.
Designed by Laura Roode. The text of this book was set in Banda.
Manufactured in the United States of America 0521 FFG 10 9 8 7 6 5 4 3 2 1
Library of Congress Cataloging-in-Publication Data
Names: Mews, Melody, author. | Stubbings, Ellen, illustrator. Title: The copycat / by Melody Mews ; illustrated by Ellen Stubbings. Description: First Little Simon paperback edition New York : Little Simon, 2021. | Series: Itty Bitty Princess Kitty ; 8 | Audience: Ages 5-9. Summary: Princess Itty likes her new classmate Tessa Tiger, but becomes frustrated and confused as Tessa begins to copy everything Itty says and does. Identifiers: LCCN 2021007449 (print) LCCN 2021007450 (ebook) | ISBN 9781534483484 (paperback) | ISBN 9781534483491 (hardcover) ISBN 9781534483507 (ebook) Subjects: CYAC: Cats—Fiction. | Princesses—Fiction. | Tigers—Fiction. | Imitation—Fiction. | Friendship—Fiction. Classification: LCC PZ7.1.M4976 Co 2021 (print) LCC PZ7.1.M4976 (eBook) | DDC [Fic]—dc23 LC record available at https://lccn.loc.gov/2021007449 LC ebook record available at https://lccn.loc.gov/2021007450

Contents

Rock Candy Rocks

Itty Bitty Princess Kitty used a miniature hammer to lightly tap on a purple rock.

Nothing happened.

"I'm not having much luck," Itty said.

"Me neither." Luna Unicorn

sighed. "But look at all *he's* got!" Luna gestured to a panda with a gigantic pile of rocks.

Well, they weren't exactly rocks. They were rock *candy*. Itty and Luna

were at Rock Candy Rocks, where the animals and other creatures of Lollyland could come to collect rock candy for themselves.

SMASH!

"He's smacking the rocks really hard and they're breaking into a million little pieces. Let's try doing that," Luna said.

"We're not supposed to hit that hard," Itty reminded her. "If a rock candy fairy sees—"

Just then, a rock candy fairy *did* see. She sped over, waving her

arms and blowing a tiny whistle.

"Uh-oh," Luna mumbled.

"Let's find a different spot," Itty whispered.

There were many types of fairies in Lollyland. One thing they all had in common was that they *loved* enforcing rules.

"That tiger has a lot of candy," Itty murmured as she and Luna walked. "Let's see what she's doing."

The tiger overheard Itty.

"I can give you some tips!" she said eagerly. "Look for the white spots on the rocks, and then tap there, like this. . . ."

She tapped gently on a nearby
rock and several chunks of candy
fell off.

"Help yourself," the tiger said.

"Wow!" said Itty. "We can't take your candy. But thanks for the tip! Maybe now we can—"

But the tiger pushed the candy toward Itty.

"Princess Itty, take it! I have *so* much candy! My mom will make me share it with my little brother anyway, and I'd rather share it with you.

I know you from school. I'm Tessa Tiger! I'm in Miss Cassidy's class, but you're in the rainbow wing, right? In Miss Sophia's class?"

Suddenly Tessa clapped a paw over her mouth.

"Sorry, sometimes I talk too much! Well, enjoy the candy! Bye!"

Then the little tiger ran away.

Itty and Luna giggled.

"She's so nice!" Luna said.

"And funny," Itty added.

The Bubble Tree

The next day Itty was at recess with Luna and her two other best friends, Chipper Bunny and Esme Butterfly. Their morning lesson had been about Lollyland geography.

"There's so much to learn," Chipper said. "But, Itty, you knew the answer to almost every question!"

"Well, as princess of Lollyland, I've had to learn the lay of the land," Itty explained. "Plus, I really do like geography."

"Hmm, I like
spelling best,"
Luna replied.
"Or maybe—"
"Geography
is my favorite
subject too!" Almost
out of nowhere, Tessa Tiger had
appeared right next to Itty.

"Hi, Tessa," Itty said. She was happy to see the young tiger again. "Esme, Chipper, this is Tessa. We met her yesterday at Rock Candy Rocks."

Esme smiled and Flipper waved.

"Hey, let's all play Turtle Tag!" Itty suggested.

"We usually use the slide as home base, but it's too crowded today," Chipper pointed out.

"We can use the bubble tree," Itty suggested, pointing to the tree on the edge of the playground.

The bubble tree was a huge tree that sent bubbles flying with the breeze.

"We're not supposed to play too close to that tree," Luna replied. "Remember? The ground around it is slippery."

Itty scratched her head. "I thought we just couldn't *climb* the tree."

"I think we're not supposed to play near it," Luna said. But she looked a little unsure.

"Itty's right. I play there all the time, and it's fine," Tessa said confidently.

"Okay, if you're sure," Luna said with a shrug.

"I'll be *it*," Chipper volunteered.

As Chipper covered his eyes and began to count, the others darted away.

Itty raced toward the swings.
Tessa followed her.

"Luna's about to get tagged!"
Tessa cried.

Itty watched as Luna ran
toward home base. Chipper was
right behind her.

"Go Luna!" Itty cheered.

But suddenly Luna wasn't running anymore . . . she was slipping and sliding! Then, with a *plop!*, she landed in a big puddle of mud.

A Dress from Moonbeam Manor

"How's your ankle?" Itty asked Luna.

Itty and Luna were walking home from school. They were walking a little slower than usual because Luna had twisted her ankle when she'd fallen during recess.

"My ankle is okay," Luna replied. "I'm more upset about my outfit! I spent an hour picking out my clothes before school today." She laughed, knowing that was sort of silly.

"I feel bad it was my idea to use the bubble tree as home base," Itty said.

"Don't worry," Luna assured her. "We couldn't remember the exact rules. And Tessa said it was fine. We probably should have just asked someone."

"Yeah," Itty said quietly.

But she was still a little mad at herself. And something else was bugging her. Did Tessa really play by the tree a lot? Or was she just saying she did? Either way, it clearly wasn't something they should be doing.

"Earth to Itty!" Luna said, waving her arms.

"Sorry!" Itty realized she hadn't been paying attention.

"Tell me about your new dress."

"Oh yeah!" Itty grinned. "It was a present from my mom. She went to Moonbeam Manor last weekend for some business, and while she was there, she got it for me."

"I've always wanted to go to Moonbeam Manor," Luna said, a bit of glitter puffing from her horn. That happened when she got excited.

Itty giggled. "My mom said there's a famous designer there, and he made the dress just for me."

"Wow." Luna sighed.

Itty continued, "It's *soooo* pretty. The bottom is blue, and the top has a moon and stars pattern."

"You're going to be the only one in Lollyland with a dress like that!" Luna said.

"A dress like what?" Itty turned and saw Tessa running behind them. She and Luna stopped so Tessa could catch up.

"My new dress that I'm going to wear tomorrow," Itty explained.

"Oh, what does it look like?" Tessa asked excitedly.

Itty described her dress to Tessa. When they reached the turn-off, Itty said goodbye to the other girls. "I hope your ankle feels better tomorrow," she told Luna. And she really meant it.

♥ chapter 4 ♥

Two of a Kind

The next morning Itty hopped off her cloud into the schoolyard. She *heard* Luna before she saw her.

"ITTY! YOUR DRESS! IT'S THE MOST BEAUTIFUL THING IN THE WORLD!"

Itty looked all around. The

schoolyard was bustling with morning drop-offs. Where was Luna? Then Itty noticed a burst of glitter. That's where Luna was, along with Chipper and Esme. Chipper was covered in glitter.

"Oopsie. Sorry." Luna giggled as she helped Chipper brush glitter off his cap. "I got really excited when I saw Itty's dress."

"Thank you." Itty smiled and twirled. Even though she was a princess, Itty didn't usually wear fancy dresses to school. But today was different. Today she was wearing a special dress—one her mom had picked out especially for her—and it felt good to show it off a little bit to her closest friends.

"It's *so* pretty," Esme said as she fluttered around Itty. "It looks just like the sky at night. I've never seen a dress like it!"

"That's because it's one of a kind," Luna said.

"Make that two of a kind," Chipper said, gesturing to Tessa . . . who was wearing a dress with a blue skirt, and a top with a moon and stars pattern.

Just like Itty's.

"We look like twins!" Tessa cried as she rushed over.

"Oh!" said Itty, startled. "Your dress . . . where did you get it?"

"I just found it," Tessa said. She was looking at the ground.

"But that dress was made specially for Itty," Luna pointed out.

"Actually . . ." Tessa looked a little embarrassed. "I made it last night. I wanted to have one just like yours, so we could match. Do you like it?"

Just then, the bell rang and it was time to go inside. Itty was glad for that. Because the truth was . . . she didn't know if she liked it.

Itty's Art Partner

Itty settled in to her desk in her classroom in the rainbow wing. It was the start of the school day, so all the desks were red. The desks in the rainbow wing changed color throughout the day. They were red first thing in the morning, and they

turned violet when it was time to
go home.

"Itty, I love your dress," Itty's
classmate Polly Porcupine said.

"Thank you," Itty replied. Usually she would have chatted with Polly more, but she didn't really feel like talking right then.

All Itty could think about was how Tessa's dress looked almost *exactly* like hers.

Sometimes, when Itty played dress-up with Luna, they wore matching outfits, and that was fun. It didn't feel fun that Tessa had matched her special dress from Moonbeam Manor, though.

It felt like Tessa was copying her.

"Today we will do a new art project," Miss Sophia said.

Itty smiled. She loved art class, and a new project sounded exciting!

Miss Sophia explained that another class would be joining them, and that each student would be paired up with a younger student from . . . Miss Cassidy's class. As she finished speaking, the door to the classroom opened and the students from Miss Cassidy's class filed in.

As Miss Sophia and Miss Cassidy began calling out the names of the pairs, Tessa raised her hand.

"May I be paired with Itty?" she asked. "We are very close friends."

"Well, you must be since your dresses are matching." Miss Sophia nodded. "Of course you may partner up."

Tessa skipped over to Itty's desk, smiling widely.

Itty tried to smile back, but she wasn't sure she was as happy about this pairing as Tessa was.

chapter 6

ART
PROJECT

Something Special!

The teachers explained the art project. Each student was to draw a picture of something that was special to them and then talk about it with their partner.

Itty arranged her crayons and markers on her desk to share with Tessa.

"You have so many colors!" Tessa exclaimed.

Itty nodded. "I love making art, so I collect markers and crayons. Help yourself to whatever colors you want."

"Is art your favorite class?" Tessa asked.

"I guess so," Itty said with a shrug.

Tessa frowned. "I thought it was geography."

Itty was confused, and then she remembered talking about geography at recess yesterday. "I like it, but it's not my favorite," she explained. "Should we start drawing?"

Itty knew what she was going to draw a picture of—her shooting star.

Itty's shooting star had arrived just in time for her to become Princess of Lollyland. She kept it in a special display case in her bedroom. Itty thought it was the most beautiful thing she had ever seen.

Itty was concentrating hard on her picture. Before she knew it, Miss Sophia was telling the class it was time to share their drawings with their partners.

Itty looked at Tessa, who had her picture turned over so Itty couldn't see it.

"Um, Tessa, are you going to turn over your picture?" Itty asked.

Hesitantly, Tessa did.

Itty looked at it. She wasn't
sure what it was. "It's nice," she
said politely. "Can you tell me
about it?"

"Um, actually, I don't know what it is," Tessa mumbled.

Itty wondered how Tessa could have drawn a picture of something special to her if she didn't know what it was. Then, as she looked more closely at Tessa's drawing, she recognized a shape.

Tessa had copied Itty's drawing.
She had drawn Itty's shooting star.

The
Copycat

"Is that my shooting star?" Itty asked Tessa.

"Um . . . is that what *you* drew?" Tessa asked.

"Yes, it is," Itty replied. "My shooting star is really special to me. It arrived just in time for me to become Princess of Lollyland."

"I remember when it happened," Tessa said eagerly. "I saw your star in the sky that night. All Lollyland saw it! It was so beautiful!"

"Thank you," Itty said slowly. "But . . . why did *you* draw a picture of *my* shooting star?"

Tessa squirmed in her chair. Itty didn't want to make her uncomfortable, but she wanted to know why Tessa had copied her picture.

"I—I just wanted our pictures to match," Tessa said finally.

"Oh," said Itty, still not understanding. The teachers had told the students to draw something that was special to them. Not something that was special to someone *else*.

Tessa looked at the floor.

Itty could tell Tessa was upset, but she wasn't sure why. Before she could ask her, Miss Cassidy announced it was time for her students to return to their classroom.

"Bye, Tessa," Itty said as the younger girl got up to leave.

Tessa waved goodbye, but Itty noticed she wasn't smiling.

♥ chapter 8 ♥

Advice from
a Queen

That night Itty was snuggled in bed, enjoying the warm glow of light coming from her shooting star, when her mom tapped on the door.

"Is it story time?" Itty asked her mom.

The Queen of Lollyland perched on the edge of Itty's bed. "Yes. We can pick up where we left off with *The Adventures of Kitty and Unicorn*," she said, referring to the story she and Itty had made up.

"Actually, Mom," Itty said, "can I talk to you about something?"
"Of course," said Queen Kitty.

Itty told her mom about Tessa—
how Tessa said it was okay to play
by the bubble tree and then how
Luna slipped and fell in the mud,
and how Tessa copied her special
dress from Moonbeam Manor, and
then copied the picture of her
shooting star in art class.

"She's a . . . she's a copycat!" Itty said finally.

"You sound pretty frustrated," the Queen replied.

"I guess I am." Itty sighed. "I just don't know why she acts like that."

"It sounds to me like Tessa really looks up to you," Itty's mom said gently. "Sometimes new friends think the only way to make someone like them is to act exactly like them."

"But I *already* like her," Itty said. "I liked her the day we met her at Rock Candy Rocks, when she showed Luna and me how to hammer the rocks just right. She was funny and nice. She even shared her candy with us."

"Maybe Tessa just needs to know that," said Itty's mother. "That you already like her. Why don't you talk to her about it?"

Later, as Itty drifted off to sleep, she decided that's exactly what she would do tomorrow: She'd talk to Tessa about it.

Talking
with Tessa

The next morning Itty looked around the schoolyard for Tessa. She spotted her heading inside the school building.

"Tessa!" Itty called, but Tessa didn't stop.

Had Tessa not heard her . . . or

had she *pretended* not to?

Later, in class, Itty's desk turned green just as the Lollyland mermaids sang twelve notes. It was time for recess. Itty and her friends went outside to the playground.

"Race you to the rainbow slide!" Chipper cried.

"I'll be there soon," Itty said. "I have to do something first."

Itty looked around and spotted
Tessa standing near the shamrock
swings. She walked over and said
hello.

Tessa looked at the ground.
"Oh, hi, Itty."

"Is something wrong, Tessa?" Itty asked. "I called to you this morning, but you didn't stop. Did you hear me?"

Tessa continued to look at the ground. "I did hear you. I just thought . . . well, I thought you probably didn't want to be my friend after I copied your drawing. And your dress. I'm sorry I was such a copycat."

"Did you copy me because you want to be my friend?" Itty asked.

Tessa nodded. "I guess so. I thought that if we liked all the same things, you'd want to be *my* friend."

Itty smiled. Her mom was right.

"My friends and I don't like all
the same things," Itty told Tessa.
"Luna's favorite ice cream flavor is
coconut, and mine is sweet cream.

I love traveling by cloud, but Esme
prefers to fly. And Chipper loves
to dance, and well . . . let's just
say dancing isn't my thing."

Tessa giggled. "How can you *not* like dancing?"

"I'm kind of terrible at it," Itty admitted.

"Oh, I love to dance," Tessa said.

"We don't have to like the same things to be friends," said Itty. She smiled at Tessa. "So, do you still want to be friends?"

"Definitely," said Tessa with a big smile.

♥ chapter 10 ♥

A Perfect Picnic!

It was a Saturday afternoon, and Chipper, and Luna were hanging out at Starfish Falls.

By then they had already gone swimming, played hide-and-seek, and searched for sea stars in the water.

Now they were having lunch. Itty had brought a basket filled with delicious foods prepared by Garbanzo, the fairy who ran the royal kitchen. All the foods Itty had brought were a big hit with her friends . . . except for one item.

"I can't believe you like roasted beets," Luna said to Itty. "They are so . . . purple!"

"They are absolutely delicious," Itty replied.

"I'm with Luna," Esme agreed, wrinkling her tiny nose. "I'll stick with the maple carrots!"

"More for me." Itty shrugged.

Just then Tessa Tiger came over. "Hi!" she said to everyone. "Thanks for inviting me to your picnic. I brought some homemade chocolate-cherry crumb cakes," she said.

"*Yum*," said Chipper, making room for Tessa to sit down.

"That sounds way better than beets," said Esme, fluttering down to the basket to take a peek.

Tessa made a face. "Beets? Yuck!"

Esme, Luna, and Chipper burst out laughing.

"I told you!" Luna exclaimed.

"You don't know what you're missing!" Itty giggled as she piled more on her plate.

.... ⌇⌇ ....
Here's a sneak peek at Itty's next royal adventure!
.... ⌇⌇ ....

Itty Bitty Princess Kitty was in her climbing room when her tummy rumbled. Itty paused. She was practicing high jumps and didn't want to stop for a snack. Her tummy rumbled again. It didn't care that Itty wanted to keep playing.

Itty jumped down and ran

toward the kitchen. Until recently Itty hadn't been allowed inside while the food fairies were cooking. But the head food fairy, Garbanzo, had relaxed her rules and sometimes allowed Itty to come in. Itty hoped this was one of those times.

"Hi, Peaches." Itty waved to a fairy wearing a chef's hat.

Peaches looked worried. "Garbanzo isn't in the best mood. . . ."

"It's okay," Itty replied. "I only want a snack."

Just then Garbanzo's loud,

squeaky voice echoed through the kitchen.

"Where are the ruby red raspberries?" Garbanzo yelled.

"We ran out," a nervous-looking fairy responded.

"Well, that is fairy terrible!" Garbanzo stomped her tiny feet. "I was planning to make the King's favorite ruby red raspberry cake!"

Garbanzo's ruby red raspberry cake was not just the King's favorite—it was Itty's favorite too!